Test # 84224

W9-ASD-325

Snow sabotage!

"Someone destroyed our beautiful sketch!" Bess exclaimed.

"We worked so hard on it!" George said in an angry voice.

Nancy tried to pick up the sketch very carefully. But it was a big, soggy mess. Hot chocolate and bunny-shaped marshmallow bits were everywhere, smearing and smudging the markings.

Who could have done such an awful thing? Nancy wondered. *Was it someone involved in the snow-sculpture contest?*

Just then Nancy got the feeling that they were being watched.

The Nancy Drew Notebooks

Available from Simon & Schuster

THE
NANCY DREW
NOTEBOOKS®

#63

Snowman Surprise

CAROLYN KEENE
ILLUSTRATED BY PAUL CASALE

Aladdin Paperbacks
New York   London   Toronto   Sydney

F
KEE

First Aladdin Paperbacks edition December 2004
Copyright © 2004 by Simon & Schuster, Inc

ALADDIN PAPERBACKS
An imprint of Simon & Schuster
Children's Publishing Division
1230 Avenue of the Americas
New York, NY 10020

The text of this book was set in Excelsior.

Printed in the United States of America.
10 9 8 7 6 5 4 3 2 1

Library of Congress Control Number 2004102674

ISBN 0-689-87411-1

7206

1

The Winter Festival

I think we should make a giant snow bunny," said eight-year-old Nancy Drew. She skipped along the sidewalk and kicked up a powdery cloud of snow.

"I think we should make a giant snow princess," said her best friend Bess Marvin. She made an outline of a big, puffy princess dress in the air.

"I think we should make a giant snow monster," George Fayne piped up. George was Bess's cousin and Nancy's other best friend. She bared her teeth like a scary monster.

"I think you girls should make a bunny, a

princess, *and* a monster," Hannah Gruen suggested with a twinkle in her eye. "It would be like a scene from a movie. The snow princess could save the snow bunny from the snow monster!"

Nancy, Bess, and George giggled. Hannah always had fun ideas. Hannah was the Drew family's housekeeper. But she had also helped take care of Nancy since she was three years old, after Mrs. Drew died.

Hannah was walking with Nancy and her friends to the neighborhood park. There was going to be a big winter festival there on Sunday. Part of the festival was a snow-sculpture contest for kids. Nancy, George, and Bess wanted to enter the contest as a team, and the applications were due today.

When the girls reached the park, Nancy thought it looked beautiful all covered with snow. The trees were covered with snow. The benches were covered with snow. Even the swing sets were covered with snow. Nancy liked the way the snow crunched under their feet and the way the cold air made their cheeks tingle. She loved winter! She especially loved winter vacation, when they could just play and not have to go to school.

The park was crowded with grown-ups and kids. Some of them were sledding or skiing on cross-country skis. Others were building snowmen and snowwomen.

"Look!" Bess said.

She pointed to a cluster of booths in one corner of the park. A sign over one of the booths said: WELCOME TO THE FIFTH ANNUAL RIVER HEIGHTS WINTER FESTIVAL.

They all headed in the direction of the booths. As they got closer, Nancy noticed a sign that said: SIGN UP HERE FOR THE SNOW-SCULPTURE CONTEST.

"That's us!" Nancy cried out. "Let's go!"

The girls ran toward the booth.

There was a young guy standing behind it. He was dressed in a silver parka with a furry collar. His long, curly red hair was tucked under an orange wool cap.

"Hey, snow artists," the guy said with a smile. "You look like you're ready to make some snow sculptures."

"Definitely!" George said eagerly.

"Well, you've come to the right place. My

name is Mad Mike. Let me give you some application forms, and we can get you started," he said.

"George and Bess and I are going to be a team," Nancy explained.

"Great idea! That means you only have to fill out one form. Have you decided what kind of sculpture you're going to make yet?" Mad Mike asked.

"A bunny!" Nancy said.

"A princess!" Bess said at the same time.

"A monster!" George chimed in.

"Whoa, a bunny-princess-monster. Sounds like a super sculpture," Mad Mike joked. "I can see it now. A fire-breathing girl with big, floppy white ears."

Nancy and her friends cracked up. "No, we're going to make just *one* of those," Nancy corrected him.

"Or we might make something else," George added.

"Well, whatever you end up making will be awesome," Mad Mike said. He handed them a form. "Just fill out this application and return it to me. You can pick a spot and get started with your sculpture whenever

5

you want. You can work on it anytime between now and Sunday. You have to be done by Sunday at noon, and the judging starts right at one."

Hannah took the application form from him. "I'll take care of that. Are there any other rules the girls should know about?"

"Hmm, rules. Yes. Absolutely no touching or tampering with other people's snow sculptures. You can use any materials you want for your snow sculpture, as long as they're not harmful to trees, grass, birds, animals, or people. And you have to be eight to enter this contest," Mad Mike said with a grin. "You girls look like you're what—twenty? Twenty-five? You should be fine."

Nancy and her friends cracked up again. Mad Mike not only had a funny nickname—*he* was funny too!

"Thanks, Mad Mike," Nancy said.

She and the others bid Mad Mike good-bye. Hannah went over to an empty booth to fill out the application form.

Nancy, Bess, and George waited nearby. They watched some kids who had already started their sculptures. Nancy recognized a couple of fourth- and fifth-graders from their school, Carl Sandburg Elementary School.

Nancy and her friends were in the third grade. They didn't see any other third graders from Carl Sandburg.

George jumped up on a snow pile, then jumped off again. "Maybe we should do a sculpture of a soccer player," she suggested. "It could be super-athletic-looking. She could be doing a header." She pretended to knock a soccer ball in the air with her head.

"How about a snow elephant?" Bess said. "We could give him a big, long trunk. Like this." She put her arm up against her face and pretended to have an elephant trunk. She swung it back and forth. "Give me peanuts!" she said in a deep voice.

Nancy liked the idea of the elephant. She also liked George's idea of doing something super-athletic-looking.

"I know," she said suddenly. "How about a ballet dancer? Ballet dancers are super-athletic!"

"Yes!" Bess cried out. "I *love* that idea! I love it even more than the elephant idea."

"Soccer players are more athletic than ballet dancers," George pointed out.

Nancy shook her head. "Ballet dancers have to jump way up in the air. They have to twirl around and around on their toes. They have to be really strong and flexible and graceful."

"Hmm, that's true," George agreed. "Okay, let's do a ballet dancer!"

"Yay!" Bess cried out. She spun around in the snow like a ballerina.

"Now, all we have to do is decide what *kind* of ballet dancer," Nancy pointed out.

"How about the Mouse King from the *Nutcracker*?" George said. "He's super-mean-looking. And he has three heads!"

"Too weird," Bess replied. "How about Aurora from *Sleeping Beauty*? We can make a snow sculpture of her sleeping!"

"Hmm," Nancy said. She liked the *Sleeping Beauty* ballet. She had seen it last year in Chicago with her father.

Then Nancy thought of another ballet she really liked. In fact, she, George, and

8

Bess had watched a video of it recently. "How about *Swan Lake*?" she suggested. "We could do a snow sculpture of Odette. Remember, she's the swan princess who falls in love with the prince?"

"Yes!" Bess said excitedly. "That's a great idea, Nancy."

George nodded. "We could do a sculpture of Odette with some of her swans."

"Yay! We're going to do a *Swan Lake* sculpture!" Nancy exclaimed.

Just then, the girls were interrupted by an angry voice.

"No, you aren't. That's *my* idea, and you stole it!"

2

A Chocolate Disaster

Nancy turned around. Standing behind them was a girl about their age. She had long, wavy brown hair that came down to her waist. She was wearing a black velvet beret, a matching black coat, and black glasses with tiny rhinestones on them.

With her was another girl who looked like her, but younger and with shorter hair. She was wearing a pink parka with fuzzy pink mittens.

"Who are you?" Nancy asked the older girl.

"I'm Denise, and you stole my idea," the girl replied huffily.

"What idea?" George asked her.

"*I* came up with the idea to do a *Swan Lake* snow sculpture *first*," Denise explained. "You girls stole it from me. I'm telling the director! You are going to get into such big, huge trouble!"

She turned to go. "Come on, Tess," she said to the younger girl.

"Where are we going?" Tess asked her. "I'm hungry, and Mommy said we could have a snack!"

Nancy realized that Tess must be Denise's younger sister.

"I'll get you a snack in a minute. But first, we have to turn in these . . . these *thieves*," Denise told Tess.

Nancy couldn't believe this was happening. "Wait a second," she called out to Denise. "How could we steal your idea? We've never even met you before."

Denise hesitated. "Well, you could have been *spying* on me and listening to me talking about my idea," she pointed out.

"We didn't spy on you. We came up with our Odette idea all by ourselves," George said firmly.

Tess tugged on Denise's sleeve. "Odette!

11

That's different from what you're doing, Didi," she said.

"Why? What are you doing?" Nancy asked Denise curiously.

Denise shrugged. "I'm doing a snow sculpture of Von Rothbart and Odile."

Nancy grinned. She remembered Von Rothbart and Odile. Von Rothbart was the evil sorcerer in *Swan Lake*. In the story, Von Rothbart put a curse on Odette and other young women so they would turn into swans between sunrise and midnight every day. Odile was his black-swan daughter who tricked Odette's true love, Prince Siegfried, into marrying her.

"That's totally different from what we're doing," Nancy told Denise. "You're doing Von Rothbart and Odile, and we're doing Odette and her swans."

"Yeah! There's no reason there can't be two *Swan Lake* sculptures in the contest, as long as they're different," George agreed.

Denise looked thoughtful. "Well, I guess," she grumbled.

Tess tugged on Denise's sleeve again.

"Can I help you with your sculpture, Didi?" she begged.

"No, Tess, you're too little," Denise replied. She smiled coolly at Nancy and her friends. "Yeah, go ahead and do your *Swan Lake* sculpture. It doesn't matter, anyway, since I'm going to win first place!"

Denise sounds pretty sure of herself, Nancy thought.

But she, George, and Bess would show her!

On Thursday morning, Nancy, George, and Bess arrived at the park bright and early. There had been a big snowstorm the night before, so the park was covered with a fresh blanket of thick, white snow.

Bess scooped up a handful of snow and patted it into a snowball. "Look out!" she cried. She aimed the snowball at George.

"Don't you dare!" George giggled.

Nancy scooped up some snow too, and joined in the fun. The girls ran around, laughing and kicking snow and throwing snowballs at each other's feet.

Nancy stopped after a few minutes,

out of breath. "Safety!" she called out.

"Me too," Bess agreed. "We should start working on our snow sculpture."

"That Denise girl is here," George said, pointing. "I guess she's doing her sculpture all by herself. She's not part of a team, like us."

Nancy looked where George was pointing. Denise was sitting on a bench, scribbling in a notebook. Her little sister, Tess, was sitting next to her.

There were other people in the park sketching and working on their sculptures too. Nancy counted at least four teams of kids and six kids working alone. She knew from the contest rules that they were all between the ages of eight and twelve.

"Now what?" Bess said.

"Why don't we make a sketch, like everybody else?" Nancy suggested. "It seems like a good idea. That way, we can plan exactly what our sculpture will look like."

"I have some drawing paper in my backpack," Bess said.

"And I have some cool markers," George added.

14

"Perfect!" Nancy said. "Let's find a place to sit."

The three girls headed over to an empty bench. They cleared off the snow and Nancy sat down. Bess handed her a drawing pad, and Nancy got to work.

They made one sketch, then another, then another. It took half a dozen tries before they got just the design they wanted.

"This is it!" Nancy announced finally. She held up the sketch.

Nancy had drawn most of it, with the other girls' help. It showed a picture of the beautiful swan princess Odette. She was wearing a white tutu and a rhinestone crown. Her arms were in the air, like wings.

Around her feet were six swans. They were looking up at her with their wings outstretched.

"Awesome!" Bess announced.

"Super awesome!" George agreed.

"Let's take a hot chocolate break," Nancy suggested. "Then we can get started on our sculpture."

"That'll be a lot of work. I think we'll need hot chocolate *and* cupcakes," Bess said.

"Good point," Nancy said with a grin.

The three girls left their sketch and their backpacks on the bench and walked over to the snack stand. Hannah had given Nancy five dollars to buy snacks for all of them.

"What can I get you girls?" asked the woman behind the counter. She had a friendly smile and lots of gray curls piled on top of her head.

"Three hot chocolates with marshmallows, please, and three cupcakes," Nancy said.

"With lots of frosting on them!" Bess added.

The woman chuckled. "You got it!"

The woman made their snacks, and Nancy paid for them. Then the girls sat down at a picnic table under the covered roof and munched on their snacks. While they ate, they watched other kids making their sculptures.

"That team over there looks like they're making a giant snow helicopter," George said, pointing.

"Or maybe it's a giant snow birthday cake," Bess frowned. "It's hard to tell."

"And look at that girl's sculpture," Nancy

said, pointing to another pile of snow. "She's making something really long and skinny."

"Maybe it'll be a snow giraffe." Bess giggled.

As soon as they were done eating, they threw away their trash and returned to the bench where they had left their backpacks and sketch.

Nancy noticed right away that something was very wrong.

"Oh, no!" she cried out. "Look at our sketch!"

Bess and George gasped. Someone had poured hot chocolate all over their drawing of Odette and the swans.

The sketch was totally ruined!

3

Trouble on Tape

"Someone destroyed our beautiful sketch!" Bess exclaimed.

"We worked so hard on it!" George said in an angry voice.

Nancy tried to pick up the sketch very carefully. But it was a big, soggy mess. Hot chocolate and bunny-shaped marshmallow bits were everywhere, smearing and smudging the markings.

Who could have done such an awful thing? Nancy wondered. *Was it someone involved in the snow-sculpture contest?*

Just then Nancy got the feeling that they were being watched. She took a deep breath and glanced around.

"Hi! Say *cheese* for the camera!"

A tall, red-haired girl was standing there, holding a video camera. She was pointing it at Nancy and her friends.

"Who are you?" Nancy asked her.

"What are you doing?" George added.

"Are you making a movie of us?" Bess piped up. She smoothed out her long blond hair and smiled right at the camera.

"I'm Joan," the girl introduced herself. "I'm doing a videotape project of the winter festival for school. Looks like you spilled something," she added, pointing to the soggy sketch.

"*We* didn't spill something. Someone *else* spilled something," George retorted. "We left for a snack break and when we came back, we found the sketch like this!"

"Who do you think did it?" Joan asked curiously. She moved toward the sketch for a close-up shot.

Nancy frowned. "Um, I don't know if

you should be putting this in your movie."

"Oh, but it's so exciting! People *love* crime!" Joan exclaimed.

Crime? Nancy wasn't sure about that. But in any case, Joan and her video camera made her kind of uncomfortable. She didn't want the whole world to know about their messed-up sketch.

Besides, Nancy realized that they needed to report what happened to the director right away.

"We have to go. We need to talk to Mad Mike," Nancy announced to Joan. She grabbed Bess and George's hands. "Come on!"

"But what about the movie?" Bess asked her.

"Come on!" Nancy insisted.

The girls found Mad Mike at a picnic table. He was eating a granola bar and looking over a pile of application forms.

"Hey, girls!" Mad Mike greeted them. "What's up? Not enough snow for you to work with?" he joked.

"We have a problem," Nancy said. Then

she proceeded to tell him about the hot chocolate incident.

Mad Mike's smile turned into a frown. "Well. That's not good at all."

"Can you find out who did it?" George asked him.

"I'll e-mail the parents and mention what happened," Mad Mike said. "It's possible someone spilled their hot chocolate by accident and is too embarrassed to say anything."

"That's true," Bess said, nodding. "It can be really embarrassing to admit you're a klutz!"

Nancy and the girls said good-bye to Mad Mike and returned to their spot. They spent the next hour redoing the sketch. Then they started working on the actual sculpture.

By the end of the afternoon, they had sculpted three swans. Nancy had to admit that they looked really great.

The sun was starting to set in the sky. "Okay, time for chili," Nancy announced, rubbing the snow off her mittens.

"Chili?" George asked her.

"Remember, you're coming over for dinner tonight? My dad is making chili!" Nancy explained.

Just then, Nancy noticed someone standing nearby. Someone with red hair.

It was Joan. She was videotaping the girls and their three swan sculptures and talking quietly into her microphone.

"Pass the cheese, please!" Nancy said.

"Pass the sour cream, please!" George added.

"Pass the hot sauce, please!" Bess chimed in.

"Hot sauce? Didn't I make the chili spicy enough for you girls?" Carson Drew joked.

Hannah took a bite of the chili and made a face. "Whew! It's definitely hot enough for me!" she said, fanning her mouth and laughing.

Mr. Drew turned to Nancy. "So how is your sculpture contest going, Pudding Pie?" he asked her. *Pudding Pie* was his special nickname for Nancy.

"Okay, except for one teeny, weeny thing," Nancy replied.

"It has to do with hot chocolate," George offered.

"And bunny-shaped marshmallows," Bess added.

"Hot chocolate? And bunny-shaped marshmallows? My, this sounds like a mystery," Mr. Drew remarked.

"It is! Sort of," Nancy replied.

She told her father and Hannah about their ruined sketch. When she was done, Mr. Drew said, "Hmm. Any suspects?"

"We hadn't thought about that," Nancy replied.

"Well, maybe it's time to start a new entry in your blue detective notebook, then," Carson suggested with a twinkle in his eye.

Nancy's face lit up. "Good idea, Daddy!"

After dinner, Nancy ran upstairs to get her detective notebook. Her father had given it to her a while ago, when she solved her first case. She used it to keep track of suspects and clues whenever she solved a mystery.

And this *was* a mystery. Someone had ruined their sketch. But who? And why?

Nancy, Bess, and George sat down in front of the fireplace in the living room with Nancy's notebook. Nancy's puppy, Chocolate Chip, lay asleep nearby. The fire felt warm and toasty. Outside, it had begun to snow lightly.

Nancy opened her notebook to a clean page. "Can anyone think of any suspects?" she asked her friends.

"Denise," Bess said immediately. "She was really mad about us making a *Swan Lake* sculpture, remember? Maybe she was mad enough to pour hot chocolate all over our brilliant sketch."

Nancy nodded. She uncapped her purple pen and began to write:

SUSPECTS:
Denise
She was mad at us for doing a *Swan Lake* sculpture.

"What about Joan?" George said suddenly. "She really wanted to put us in her movie. She asked a lot of questions about the sketch."

26

"But why would Joan pour hot chocolate on our sketch?" Bess asked her.

George grinned. "So she'd have something exciting to put in her movie, silly! Maybe her movie was super boring, and she wanted to make it interesting."

"Hmm," Bess said.

Nancy thought that George had a point. Under Denise's name, she wrote:

Joan
Maybe she ruined our sketch so she could make her movie more exciting.

Nancy closed her notebook. "You know, maybe Mad Mike was right. Maybe it was an accident, and the person is too embarrassed to say anything."

"Maybe," George agreed. "I hope so. I don't want anything else to happen to our sculpture!"

The next morning, Nancy, Bess, and George arrived at the park bright and early to work on their sculpture. It was already Friday, and the competition was in just two days.

They still had to make three more swans. They also had to make Odette herself. She would be the hardest part!

The park was already filled with kids working on their sculptures. Nancy and her friends headed for their own sculpture area. It was a big, flat spot between two tall oak trees.

On their way, they passed Denise and Tess.

"Hi!" Denise called out. "How's your sculpture going?" Nancy thought Denise had a smirk on her face.

"Oh, fine," Nancy said casually. "How's yours going?"

"Awesome," Denise replied smugly. "It's pretty obvious who's going to win first place."

"Oh, *really*?" Bess snapped. "Just because some people need to spill hot chocolate all over the place to make sure they win—"

Nancy elbowed Bess. "Shhhh!" she whispered.

"Huh?" Denise frowned.

Tess glanced up at her big sister. She looked confused and upset. "What's she talking about, Didi?" she asked Denise.

"Come on." Nancy yanked Bess by the arm and pulled her away. "Bye, Denise! Bye, Tess."

"Why did you drag me away?" Bess asked Nancy. "She was on the verge of confessing!"

"We don't have any proof that Denise is the one," Nancy told Bess.

Bess shrugged. "She acts so guilty, though!"

Nancy, Bess, and George soon reached the two tall oak trees.

Then Nancy stopped in her tracks. Their sculpture was . . . gone!

Someone had smashed the three snow swans—and in their place were three yellow rubber duckies!

4

The Bunny Clue

"Oh, no!" Bess cried out. "Someone totally destroyed our swans!"

"This is awful," Nancy said. She had to hold back tears. "I can't believe someone could do that to our swans."

"Look at the rubber duckies!" George exclaimed. "Someone is playing a prank on us."

"Maybe the person left a clue," Nancy said hopefully.

She bent down and began searching the area carefully. There were footprints in the snow, but they were all different sizes and jumbled together. She couldn't pick out anyone's footprints in particular.

Aside from the footprints, there were no clues. Nancy stood up and brushed her snow-covered mittens against her coat.

"Okay, so now we know the hot chocolate wasn't an accident," Nancy announced. "Let's go tell Mad Mike right away."

"Definitely!" Bess agreed.

Nancy and her friends rushed over to Mad Mike. He was helping one of the other teams with their sculpture. The sculpture looked like a cross between a sheep and a motorcycle.

"Mad Mike!" Nancy called out.

Mad Mike turned around. "Hey, girls! What's up?" he said with a friendly smile.

"Someone ruined our swans!" Bess announced.

"What?" Mad Mike frowned.

Nancy told him what had happened. When she was finished, Mad Mike looked just like his name: *mad.*

"Well, girls, that's terrible. Let's see if we can find out who was responsible," Mad Mike said.

He pulled a whistle out of his coat pocket

and blew it, hard. The sound was really loud. Nancy covered her ears. So did George and Bess.

Mad Mike cupped his hands over his mouth. "Everybody please gather around," he called out. "We need to have an emergency meeting!"

The other kids stopped what they were doing and came running over. Denise and Tess were among them. Denise gave Nancy a curious look.

"These three girls are making a *Swan Lake* sculpture," Mad Mike announced to the crowd. "But someone messed up their sculpture. And maybe that same someone messed up their sketch yesterday."

The kids in the crowd looked at each other. There was a long silence.

"If anyone knows anything about this, I'd like them to come forward," Mad Mike went on.

No one came forward.

Mad Mike sighed. "Fine. If anyone would like to come forward on their own later and talk in private, I'm here. Needless to say, this kind of behavior is against all our rules here at the winter festival. Further incidents will not be tolerated!"

Nancy glanced around at the faces in the crowd. Everyone was staring at Nancy, George, and Bess.

Then she noticed that Denise had a smile on her face.

What's that all about? Nancy wondered.

Then Nancy noticed something else.

Joan was filming the whole thing on her video camera.

Bess scooped up a handful of snow, then another. Then she dumped all the snow on the ground and began molding it into a shape.

"Is that a swan?" Nancy asked her. She was in the middle of making her second swan. It had a long, graceful neck and two wide wings stretching into the air.

Bess shook her head. "Nope. I'm making a little snow cave for the rubber duckies."

"That's really nice, Bess, but we have to get busy!" George scolded her. She was on her knees, molding Odette's legs.

"Okay, okay, I'm done," Bess replied. She

patted the snow into a cave shape and tucked the rubber ducks deep inside. "Now they'll be nice and cozy."

"We have to work extra hard to solve this case," Nancy told the girls as she carved ridges into the wings, to look like feathers. "The competition is Sunday. We don't want anything else to go wrong with our sculpture between now and then!"

"I still think it's that girl with the video camera," George said. She glanced over her shoulder at Joan, who was videotaping some kids working on a seagull sculpture.

"I still think it's Denise," Bess piped up. "She doesn't want *our Swan Lake* sculpture to beat *her Swan Lake* sculpture!"

"We don't have any proof against either Joan or Denise, though," Nancy pointed out. "We don't even have any clues yet."

"I think this is the toughest mystery we've ever faced, Nancy," George said.

Nancy nodded. "I think so, too."

After a while, the girls finished four of the six swans as well as Odette's legs. Nancy suggested that they take a hot chocolate break.

"Why don't you and I go to the snack stand, Bess? George, you stay here and guard the sculpture. We'll bring you back some hot chocolate," Nancy said.

"Good idea," George agreed. She crossed her arms over her chest. She scrunched up her face and made herself look tough and mean. "I won't let anyone come near it!"

Nancy giggled. "We'll be right back."

She and Bess made their way over to the snack stand. The same woman from yesterday was standing behind the counter.

"More hot chocolate and cupcakes, girls?" she asked them with a friendly smile.

"Just hot chocolate today, thank you!" Nancy said. She and the others were still full from lunch. "Three of them. We're taking one back to our friend George."

"Three hot chocolates, coming right up!" the woman said.

She prepared the hot chocolate, added marshmallows, and set the cups down on the counter. Just then, Nancy noticed something.

"The marshmallows," Nancy said, pointing to the cups. "They're round."

The woman nodded. "That's right."

"They're not bunny-shaped," Nancy went on.

The woman chuckled. "Bunny-shaped? No. We don't have bunny-shaped marsh-mallows here."

"Have you *ever* had them?" Nancy asked her. "Like, maybe yesterday?"

The woman shook her head. "No, we've never had them here. Not yesterday, not ever. Not since I've been working here, anyway."

Nancy turned to Bess. "This is a major clue for our case!" she whispered excitedly.

5
More Competition

A major clue for our case?" Bess repeated. "What do you mean?"

"I mean, I was sort of assuming that the hot chocolate that was dumped on our sketch was from this snack stand," Nancy explained. "But *that* hot chocolate had bunny-shaped marshmallows in it. It was *special* hot chocolate!"

Bess's blue eyes sparkled. "Oh!"

"Now, all we have to do is figure out who drinks hot chocolate with bunny marshmallows in it," Nancy pointed out.

"Yes! And then the case will be solved," Bess agreed.

"Maybe. Let's go back and tell George!" Nancy said.

Nancy paid the woman for the hot chocolates. Then she and Bess headed back to their sculpture station, carrying their cups carefully.

Nancy's thoughts were racing. Was *this* the big break in their case that they had been waiting for?

"Hi! We're taking a survey on what kind of hot chocolate people are drinking today," Nancy said cheerfully.

"We're going to write an article about it for our school paper," George explained. She held up her notebook and pen.

Nancy and George were talking to three boys who were making a Mount Rushmore snow sculpture. The boys glanced up curiously.

"A hot chocolate survey?" one of the boys said. "I don't even *like* hot chocolate."

"I'm allergic to milk," another boy said.

"I like hot cider way better," the third boy piped up.

"Okay, thank you," Nancy said.

George leaned over to Nancy. "Let's try the next group," she whispered.

After leaving the snack bar, Nancy and Bess had told George about their exciting new marshmallow clue. George had suggested that they figure out a clever way to find out who in the competition drank hot chocolate with bunny marshmallows.

Bess had come up with the idea for the pretend survey. They could go around and ask the other kids in the park what kind of hot chocolate they liked.

George and Nancy had decided to conduct the survey. Bess had agreed to stay behind to guard Odette and the swans.

"There's Denise," George whispered to Nancy. "She's one of our main suspects so far. Let's go talk to her."

Nancy nodded. "If she drinks hot chocolate with bunnies in it, then she's probably the guilty one!"

"Definitely," George agreed.

Nancy and George walked over to the spot where Denise was working on her sculpture. Nancy had to admit that Denise's sculpture looked really awesome so far. Von Rothbart looked like a scary cross between a man and an owl. Denise had also started to work on Von Rothbart's evil swan-daughter, Odile.

Nancy was about to call out to Denise. Then she clamped her mouth shut. Denise and Tess seemed to be having an argument. Nancy wanted to hear what they were arguing about.

Nancy put her finger up to her lips. "Shhh," she said to George. "Over here!"

Nancy led George over to a nearby tree. The two girls hid behind it and listened.

"But it's not fair that Mommy is taking you to Chicago to see *Swan Lake* and not me," Tess was complaining.

"Mom's taking me as a reward for being in the sculpture contest," Denise explained.

"But why can't I go too?" Tess demanded.

"You're not in the contest."

"But why can't I be in the contest?"

"Because you're too young! You have to be at least eight. You're only six."

"Six and three quarters!" Tess corrected her.

"Besides, I don't need any help and Dad's

taking you someplace fun while Mom and I are in Chicago," Denise said.

"Not fair! I want to go to *Swan Lake* with you and Mommy," Tess pouted. "What if I helped you with your sculpture? Then maybe Mommy would take me, too," she said hopefully.

Denise sighed. "I don't want your help, Tess. I have to make my sculpture perfect so I win first prize."

All of a sudden, Denise seemed to realize that Nancy and George were standing behind the tree. "What are you doing?" Denise snapped. "Are you eavesdropping again?"

"Eaves—*what*?" Tess said, looking confused.

"Eaves*dropping*. It means they're listening to other people's conversations when they're not supposed to," Denise replied.

"We're not eavesdropping!" Nancy reassured her. "We just came by to, um, say hi. And see how your sculpture's going."

"Well, as you can see, it's going fine," Denise said in a grumpy voice.

Nancy walked over to the sculpture. She noticed there were two steaming cups of some sort of beverage next to them.

Was it hot chocolate? Nancy wondered. She pretended to check out the sculpture. But instead, she peered into the cups.

They were filled with hot cider. Nancy bit back her disappointment.

"Okay, we'll be going now," Nancy said to Denise and Tess. "Bye!"

George looked puzzled. "But, Nancy, our survey—"

Nancy tugged on George's arm. "It's okay. Bye, Denise and Tess!" she called out.

Nancy and George moved on. "Why didn't we ask them about what kind of hot chocolate they're drinking?" George whispered.

"Because they were drinking hot cider. Come on, let's check out the next person," Nancy whispered back.

Down the path from Denise, a girl was making a snow sculpture of a race car. "Oh, wow, that's so cool!" George said to the girl. "Is that a Nascar race car?"

"Grand Prix," the girl corrected her. "I'm a huge Grand Prix fan."

The girl seemed a little older than Nancy and George. She was dressed in a black parka. Her dark brown hair hung down in dozens of dreadlocks with red and yellow beads in them.

"I'm Layah," the girl introduced herself.

"I'm Nancy, and this is George," Nancy said. "Your sculpture is really great!"

"What are you guys making for the competition?" Layah asked.

"We're making a scene from *Swan Lake,*" George replied. "We're on a team with my cousin Bess."

"Oh, you're the ones who had your sculpture messed up," Layah said. "That's too bad. Maybe you should make something else, anyway. Ballet is kind of lame."

"Lame?" George burst out.

Layah shrugged. "Yeah. You put on a pink tutu and spin around. Big deal! Now, Grand Prix racing—*that's* exciting!"

"Ballet is *way* more exciting!" George shot back. "You have to be super strong to do jumps and leaps. And I bet race-car drivers can't do splits in the air, like ballet dancers do!"

"Oh, yeah?" Layah snapped.

As the two girls argued back and forth, Nancy happened to notice something.

There was a cup of hot chocolate sitting next to Layah's backpack.

It had bunny-shaped marshmallows in it!

6

The Disappearing Ducks

Nancy looked again, just to make sure. Sure enough, there were four . . . five . . . six bunny-shaped marshmallows floating around in Layah's hot chocolate.

Nancy leaned over to George and whispered, "Check out Layah's hot chocolate."

"Huh?" George whispered back. She craned her neck to look. "Oh!"

"What's so interesting?" Layah asked Nancy and George curiously. "What are you two whispering about?

"We were just noticing your hot chocolate," Nancy said with a smile. "It looks really yummy. Where did you get it?"

"That place around the corner," Layah

replied. "It's called Sun something . . . no, Star something . . . no, Moon! That's it. Moon's Deli."

"I've never heard of it," George said.

"It's new, I think," Layah said.

"Do you go there a lot?" Nancy asked her.

Layah shook her head. "Today was the first time. My mom took me there before we came here. She had to pick up some eggs or milk or whatever."

Nancy tried to figure out if Layah might be lying. What if today wasn't the first time Layah went to Moon's Deli? What if she went there on Wednesday, bought some hot chocolate with bunny marshmallows, then brought it back to the park?

And what if that hot chocolate ended up all over the girls' *Swan Lake* sketch?

Could Layah *be our culprit?* Nancy wondered.

"We have to add Layah to the suspect list," Bess said. She slipped off her pink bunny slippers and sat down cross-legged on her sleeping bag.

"I agree," George piped up. She lay her sleeping bag down between Bess's and Nancy's.

Nancy, Bess, and George were having a sleepover at Nancy's house. They had everything they needed: sleeping bags, pillows, games, and toys.

There was also a tray of goodies from Hannah: a big bowl of buttery popcorn, homemade sugar cookies, potato chips, and mugs of hot chocolate. The hot chocolate had regular old marshmallows in them, though, not bunny marshmallows.

Nancy was wearing her favorite pajamas. They had tiny red roses on them. Bess was wearing pink pajamas that matched her bunny slippers. George was wearing blue pajamas with big green polka dots.

Nancy got her special detective notebook from her desk. She opened it to the page about their sculpture.

She uncapped her purple pen. In the Suspects column, under Denise and Joan's names, she wrote:

Layah
She was drinking hot chocolate with
bunny marshmallows in it.

Nancy stopped writing and glanced up.
"Why would Layah want to mess up our
sculpture, though?"

Bess shrugged. "Maybe she doesn't want
us to win," she guessed.

"She *did* say ballet was lame," George
reminded Nancy. "Maybe she didn't want
our ballet sculpture to beat her race-car
sculpture."

Nancy thought about this. "If that's true,
she would have messed up Denise's sculpture too. Denise is doing a ballet sculpture
too," she pointed out.

"Hmm," George said slowly. "But maybe
Layah doesn't *know* about Denise's sculpture."

Bess took a fistful of popcorn and
munched on it. "I still think it's Denise," she
said, chewing. "Did you see that mean, nasty
smile on her face when Mad Mike told everybody that our sculpture was destroyed?"

Nancy circled Denise's name on the

suspect list. She also circled Joan's name, just below. "Joan is still a suspect too."

"Yeah!" George said. "She's always hanging around. She likes to film all the bad stuff that happens to us."

"The only clue we have is the bunny marshmallows," Nancy reminded her friends.

"I know!" George said suddenly. "I just thought of a really cool plan."

"What?" Nancy asked her curiously.

"I'll bring my camera to the park tomorrow—the one I got for my birthday," George explained. "I'll secretly take some photos of Denise and Joan and Layah. My dad can print them out. Then we can bring the photos to Moon's Deli and ask the owner if any of them was in Moon's Deli on Wednesday."

"That's a great idea!" Bess said eagerly.

"That's a really, *really* great idea," Nancy agreed.

Nancy liked George's plan. They *had* to catch whoever was responsible for everything as soon as possible. The competition was the day after tomorrow. They couldn't let anything else happen to their sculpture!

* * * *

On Saturday morning, Nancy, Bess, and George walked over to the park right after breakfast. The three of them were bundled in their parkas, hats, and mittens. Their boots made crunching sounds in the snow.

On Friday, the girls had completed all six swans and most of Odette. Now, they had to finish making her.

Mr. Drew had made them a big stack of blueberry pancakes before they left the house. "You'll need lots of energy to finish your sculpture today!" he had said.

Full of blueberry pancakes, Nancy and her friends made their way through the park. Squirrels and birds skittered out of their way. The park was already bustling with activity. Lots of kids were there, including Denise, Tess, and Layah.

Mad Mike was also there, checking out everyone's sculptures. Joan was trailing behind him with her video camera.

Nancy felt nervous. What if the person who had wrecked their sculpture on Friday had wrecked it again? There would be no time to fix it before the next day's competition!

The girls soon reached their sculpture. Nancy let out a sigh of relief. The sculpture was standing there, safe and sound.

"Whew!" George said.

"No one touched the swans!" Bess exclaimed. She knelt down in the snow and inspected them. "Not a scratch. And Odette looks perfect too."

"She just needs arms and a head," George joked.

"Ha-ha," Nancy laughed.

Then Bess gasped. "Oh, no!"

"What is it, Bess?" Nancy asked her worriedly.

"Remember the little snow cave I made for the rubber duckies?" Bess cried out.

"Yeah," George said.

"They're not in there any more!" Bess exclaimed. "Someone stole the rubber duckies!"

7

The Crowning Touch

"**S**omeone stole the rubber duckies?" Nancy repeated.

"Why would anyone do *that*?" George said, puzzled.

"I don't know, but they're not here!" Bess moaned. "Poor duckies!"

"Maybe some boy or girl was walking by here, saw the ducks, and decided to take them," George pointed out.

Nancy shook her head. "The ducks were all the way inside their snow cave. There's no way someone could have seen them unless they were really, really looking."

"That's true," George said.

Nancy glanced around. Everyone was busy working on their sculptures. No one seemed to be watching Nancy and her friends, not even Joan. Joan was videotaping some kids nearby who were making a snow sculpture of the Empire State Building.

"This doesn't make sense," Nancy said after a while. "Did the same person who spilled hot chocolate on our sketch and messed up the three swans steal the ducks too? And why?"

"You're right," Bess agreed. "It doesn't make sense at all. It's not like the rubber duckies are valuable or anything. Even though they *are* super adorable!"

Nancy frowned. "Maybe we should just forget about the rubber ducks for now. We really need to finish our sculpture."

"Why don't you two finish up Odette?" George suggested. "While you're doing that, I can take secret pictures of our suspects with my camera." On the way to the park, the three girls had swung by George's house to pick up her camera.

"Sounds good!" Nancy said, nodding.

"Hey, guys? I have a surprise," Bess said suddenly.

"A surprise?" Nancy grinned.

Bess pulled something out of her parka pocket. It was a silver crown with rhinestones and white feathers on it.

"I found this in my costume trunk yesterday," Bess announced. "I thought it would be perfect for Odette."

"Cool!" George exclaimed.

Nancy smiled. "It's beautiful."

Nancy could just imagine Odette with a white feather crown surrounded by six graceful swans. It was going to be really awesome!

George got her camera out of her backpack. Then she waved good-bye. "I'm off to do some detective work!"

"Good luck!" Nancy said, waving back.

After George left, Nancy and Bess started working on Odette. The two girls dragged over a bench so they could have something to stand on.

Nancy took a big handful of snow and started sculpting Odette's right arm. Bess worked on Odette's left arm. The fingers were the hardest part. The snow kept breaking up and falling off.

But Nancy was patient. Finally she was done with the right arm. A few minutes later, Bess finished up the left arm.

After the arms were done, Nancy and Bess worked on Odette's head together.

"Should we make Odette smile?" Bess asked Nancy.

"Maybe a sad smile. She's sad because she's under a terrible spell," Nancy reminded Bess.

"That's true," Bess said. "It sure would be really lame if we turned into swans every morning at dawn."

Nancy nodded. "*Really* lame!"

The girls finally finished Odette's head. Odette had two big eyes, a long, slender nose, and a sad-looking smile. Her hair was arranged up on her head, ballerina-style.

Bess stood on her tiptoes on the bench and put the white-feather crown on Odette's hair.

"She's so pretty!" Bess sighed.

"She's totally perfect," Nancy agreed.

George showed up just then. "Hey, our

sculpture looks great!" she said excitedly.

"Did you get the photos?" Nancy asked her.

George nodded. "It wasn't easy. I got Layah's picture first. She was so busy working on her sculpture that she didn't notice me. But Denise almost caught me. So did Joan."

"Wow," Bess said. "Good detective work, George!"

"I'll get my dad to print them out on our computer tonight. Then we can go to Moon's Deli tomorrow morning and show the photos to the owner," George said.

"Definitely," Nancy said. "Thank you, George!"

But inside, Nancy was worried. Would tomorrow morning be too late? Would the culprit try to mess up their sculpture before the competition?

"Hi! Say cheese for the camera!"

Nancy whirled around. Joan was standing nearby, videotaping them.

"So! How do you feel about tomorrow's competition?" Joan called out. "Talk loudly for the microphone!"

"Uh, fine," Nancy replied. She hoped Joan

hadn't overheard them discussing the photos.

"Aren't you worried something else is going to happen to your sculpture? You've had a lot of bad luck lately," Joan went on.

"No, nothing's going to happen to our sculpture!" Bess burst out.

Joan clicked off her camera and smiled. "If you say so," she said.

Nancy watched Joan as she walked away. Was George right? Was Joan the guilty one?

On Sunday morning Nancy, George, Bess, and Hannah went to Moon's Deli. It was right around the corner from the park. It was a small pink building with a purple door. Next to the words *Moon's Deli* was a big painting of a crescent moon.

The four of them went inside.

"You have the photos, right?" Nancy asked George.

George nodded. "They're right here in my backpack."

Hannah squeezed Nancy's hand. "It's so much fun coming along with you when you're doing detective work," she whispered. "I feel like a detective too!"

Nancy squeezed back. "I'm so glad you could come with us, Hannah!"

"Can I help you ladies?"

A man appeared behind the counter. He had silvery-gray hair and a big silvery-gray beard. He was wearing a purple T-shirt with moons and stars on it.

"I'd like to order these girls some sandwiches for lunch," Hannah told the man with a friendly smile. "Ham and cheese okay?" she asked the girls.

"Yes, please!" the three girls said all together.

"Ham and cheese coming right up," the man replied.

While the man was making the sandwiches, George slipped her photos out of her backpack. She held them to the man. "Do you recognize any of these girls?" she asked him.

"Have any of them been to your store lately?" Nancy added.

The man chuckled. "What are you girls, detectives?"

Hannah laughed. "Sort of! They're trying to find somebody."

"I see," the man said, nodding.

He began sorting through the photos. "She was here," he said, pointing to the photo of Layah.

"When?" Bess asked him.

"Friday," the man replied.

"Any other day?" Nancy asked him eagerly.

The man shook his head. "Friday was the only time I can recall. And I'm here every day."

Nancy frowned. Maybe Layah *had* been telling the truth.

The man flipped to the next photo. It was the photo of Joan. "Nope, I've never seen her before," he said.

Nancy sighed. In her mind, Joan had been creeping up to the top of the suspects list.

Then the man got to the photo of Denise. "Oh, yes, she's been here," he said slowly. "On Thursday. No, on Wednesday! I remember that because my hot chocolate machine broke that morning. I got it fixed just before this girl came in."

Nancy and her friends exchanged a glance. "Did this girl order hot chocolate?" Nancy asked the man.

He nodded. "Sure thing. Extra-large, with bunny marshmallows."

"Really?" Nancy said excitedly.

"Really. Now, I'd better get back to those ham and cheese sandwiches," the man said with a grin.

Nancy turned to George and Bess. "I think we have our culprit!" she whispered.

"Was I right, or what?" Bess exclaimed.

"You were right, Bess! Now, all we have to do is get her to confess," Nancy said.

As soon as Hannah had paid for the sandwiches, the four of them walked around the corner to the park. Nancy had to force herself not to break into a run. She couldn't wait to confront Denise.

They had found their culprit just in time. It was five minutes till twelve. The winter festival—and the judging for the snow-sculpture competition—was starting in one hour!

The girls and Hannah crossed the park. There was a huge blue banner that stretched between two maple trees. It said: WELCOME TO THE FIFTH ANNUAL RIVER HEIGHTS WINTER FESTIVAL.

The park was filled with people. Everyone was walking around and admiring the snow sculptures.

"Denise's sculpture is over there," Nancy said, pointing.

On the way, she and the girls passed their own *Swan Lake* sculpture. Nancy was relieved to see that it was still standing. Maybe Denise had been scared of getting caught.

Then Nancy did a double take.

Odette's head was bare. Bess's white-feather crown was missing!

8

The Thief Is Found

"Odette's crown is gone!" Nancy exclaimed.

Bess, George, and Hannah stopped in their tracks. Bess rushed up to the sculpture of Odette. "Denise took my crown!" she cried out. "She's not going to get away with this!"

"Let's go get the crown back from her," George agreed.

Nancy and her friends ran over to Denise's sculpture, followed by Hannah. Denise was smoothing a feather on one of Von Rothbart's owl wings. Tess was sitting on the bench, watching her big sister. Her legs were swinging back and forth, kicking at a small mound of snow.

"Hey, Denise!" Nancy called out.

Denise stopped what she was doing and turned around. She frowned when she saw Nancy and the others. "What do you want? I'm busy!" Denise replied.

Bess put her hands on her hips. "Give me back my crown!" she demanded.

"Your . . . what?" Denise said. She looked confused. "I don't know what you're talking about."

"Yes, you do," Bess insisted. "You poured hot chocolate all over our sketch. You wrecked three of our swans. You left three rubber duckies in their place, *then* you stole the rubber duckies back. And finally, you stole my crown!"

Denise's jaw dropped. "You're crazy! I didn't do any of those things!" she protested.

"Yeah, leave my sister alone!" Tess piped up.

Nancy glanced over at Tess.

And then Nancy noticed something.

There was a single white feather poking out of the pocket of Tess's parka.

"Tess, what's sticking out of your pocket?" Nancy said slowly. "Did you do all those things?"

Denise, Bess, and George all turned around and stared at Tess. Tess stuffed her hands into her pockets. She looked around, like she wanted to escape.

"Tess?" Denise said finally. "What are they talking about? Is this true?"

Tess's lips started to quiver. "Y-yes," she said in a trembling voice. "But please don't tell Mommy and Dad!"

Denise walked over to her little sister and wrapped her arm around her shoulders. "What happened?" she asked her gently.

"I really, really wanted you to win, Didi," Tess admitted. "I took your hot chocolate when you weren't looking and spilled it all over their swan picture. I squished their three snow swans and put my bath duckies there. I thought that would trick them! But then I missed my duckies, so I took them back."

"And what about the crown?" Denise asked her.

Tess pulled the crown out of her pocket. "I thought if I took it, their ballerina sculpture would be ugly. And then you'd win for sure."

Tears rolled down Tess's pink cheeks. "I really, really wanted to help you win, Didi!

I thought then maybe I could go to Chicago with you and Mommy and see *Swan Lake*."

"Oh, Tess," Denise said in a sad-sounding voice. She gave her sister a hug.

Tess hugged Denise back. Then she handed the crown to Bess. "I'm really, really sorry," she apologized.

"No, *I'm* the one who should say I'm sorry," Denise told Nancy and her friends. "I wouldn't let Tess help me with my sculpture. If I had, she wouldn't have done all those bad things."

Nancy glanced at Bess and George. Neither of them looked mad anymore. "That's okay," Nancy said, finally.

"Yeah," Bess and George said in unison.

Hannah put her hand on Nancy's shoulder. "That's very big of you girls."

"Say cheese for the camera!"

Nancy turned around. Joan was standing there, videotaping all of them.

"What did I miss?" Joan asked everybody.

Nancy smiled at Denise. "You didn't miss anything," she said to Joan.

Denise smiled back gratefully.

* * * *

Mad Mike stood up on the snow-covered podium. A big crowd gathered around him.

"And the winner of the snow-sculpture contest is . . ." Mad Mike began.

He grinned and peered around at the crowd. He seemed to enjoy drawing out the suspense.

Nancy squeezed George and Bess's hands. The cousins squeezed back. *Who's going to be the winner?* Nancy wondered.

"Good luck, girls," Hannah whispered.

"No matter who wins, I'm proud of all of you," Mr. Drew added. He had arrived just in time for the judging.

"The winner is the *Swan Lake* scene by Nancy Drew, George Fayne, and Bess Marvin!" Mad Mike announced.

Nancy, Bess, and George began jumping up and down in the air. "Yay!" they all cried out.

Denise came up to them. "Congratulations," she said. "You guys deserved to win. I know I gave you a super hard time. But you guys definitely deserved to win."

"Thanks," Nancy told her.

"And now, for second place," Mad Mike went on. "The judges had a hard time deciding on second place. There were some close contenders. But in the end, they made their decision. Second place goes to another *Swan Lake* sculpture, by Denise Eliopoulos!" he announced.

Denise's eyes got enormous. "I . . . I won second place?" she stammered.

"Congratulations!" George told her.

Tess came running up to her sister, followed by a man and a woman dressed in matching silver parkas. Nancy guessed that they were Denise and Tess's parents. "Yay, Didi!" Tess screamed. "You won! You won!"

"Congratulations, honey," Mrs. Eliopoulos told her daughter. "Good job!"

Denise turned to her parents. "Mom? Dad? Can we take Tess to Chicago to see *Swan Lake* with us, as a special treat?" she begged.

Mr. and Mrs. Eliopoulos exchanged a glance. "Of course, honey," Mr. Eliopoulos said. "That's a nice idea. That's very generous of you."

Tess hugged her sister. "Thank you, Didi!"

"Now, that gives *me* an idea," Carson piped up. He turned to Nancy. "Why don't I take you three girls to *Swan Lake* too? It'll

be my reward to you for being such great sculptors!"

"And great detectives," Hannah added.

Nancy giggled. "Thanks, Daddy! We'd love to go. Wouldn't we, George and Bess?"

"Definitely!" George exclaimed.

"What should I wear?" Bess added.

"Hey, winners! Say cheese for the camera!"

Nancy turned around. Joan was standing there, pointing her video camera at them.

This time, Nancy decided that it would be okay to pose for Joan's movie. In fact, it would be pretty awesome!

She, Bess, George, Denise, and Tess stood next to each other, faced Joan, and smiled big, happy smiles for the camera.

Mystery solved!

That night before going to bed, Nancy got her diary out of her desk. She put on her pajamas, curled up in bed, and opened the diary to a fresh page.

She wrote:

Yay! Today George, Bess, and I won first place for our *Swan Lake* snow sculpture.

We were afraid we wouldn't be able to enter the contest because someone kept trying to mess up our sculpture the whole time. The person turned out to be Tess, Denise's little sister. Tess wanted to help Denise, but she was too young to enter and Denise really didn't want her hanging around. So Tess tried to help secretly by wrecking our sculpture. That way, Denise would have a better chance of winning first prize.

It would have been cool if Denise and her sister could have worked as a team, just like George and Bess and I worked as a team. It's fun to win first prize. But it's even more fun to share first prize with other people, like your friends and family.

Denise finally figured that out. She invited her sister to go to Chicago to see *Swan Lake* with her. So now they'll get to share that!

Case closed!

REDISCOVER THE CLASSIC MYSTERIES OF NANCY DREW